Ajala the Terrible Child

& other stories

By Rotimi Ogunjobi

Rotimi Ogunjobi

Auntie Mimie Children Series

© 2013 Rotimi Ogunjobi

ISBN: 978-978-49837-0-9

Rotimi Ogunjobi

AUTHOR'S ACKNOWLEDGEMENT

Some of the stories in this book were adapted from several Yoruba folk tales including from the books previously written in Yoruba by D. O. Fagunwa.

Purchase Enquiries:

Xceedia (Media and Publishing) Ltd

publishing@xceedia.co.uk

CONTENTS

Rotimi Ogunjobi

USMAN AND THE LEOPARD

Usman, a farmer, was walking one morning through a bush path which led to his farm. As he got close to a village which was along the way he found Leopard inside a steel cage. The cage was a trap which had been set by the people living in a nearby village, and the cage had been made in such a way that once an animal entered, it would be unable to get out again unless the door was opened from outside. Leopard was hopelessly trapped.

'Open the door of this horrible cage for me, my good man,' Leopard desperately pleaded; but Usman refused. Leopard begged for long, and still Usman would not open the cage.

'What is it that I have done to you?' Leopard unhappily said. 'Do you not know that I could one day be of help to you too? It is true that everyone calls me a dangerous animal, but I know that this is not true. You know how wicked human beings are and how they hate one another, and speak evil against one another. If you live with me for only three days, you will never want to leave my home because you will see how pleasant I really am. Certainly, if you go away and you leave me in this cage, someone else will soon come along in a moment to release me. You should then pray that our paths never cross again, but it certainly will, one day.'

And when Usman heard this he said to Leopard:

'What you say is true; I even understand the little that you have not said. However, I cannot help but be afraid. If I free you, and then you attack me and tear me to pieces, how wise would I then have been?'

'I give my word that I will do you no harm. But hurry because time is precious,' Leopard said to him. Leopard was so persuasive, and so Usman went to the cage and opened the door. But no sooner had Leopard come out of the cage that he held him by the neck and made to kill him; but Usman pleaded with Leopard.

'Be patient with me,' Usman said. 'Let us bring this matter to be heard by five persons, and then we should abide by their judgment.' Leopard grudgingly agreed, and together they walked on along the bush path.

They soon met Goat, and Usman told Goat what had happened. He told Goat how he had seen Leopard in a cage, how Leopard had pleaded to be released, and how against wise judgment he had shown mercy only to be now at the risk of becoming Leopard's dinner. After he had finished his story, Goat turned to Leopard and said:

'These human beings are wicked and full of lies. Ever since my owner bought me, I have had nothing but misery. When I have kids I care for them all by myself. And when they are grown up, he seizes them and sells them away. All I get every day is a few unripe bananas in the morning, and then I have to go out to find leaves to eat for the rest of the day. I rarely get any yams or corn meal. And when he has eaten and has drunk some wine, he takes a stick and beats me soundly, all for his pleasure. Human beings are no good at all; Leopard must surely eat this one.' And after Goat had said this, Leopard again made to kill Usman but the man quickly reminded him of their agreement.

'Five persons must listen to this, we've seen only one so far,' he said.

And so they continued on through the bush path. They soon met Horse, and again Usman told Horse what had happened, while Leopard waited impatiently and watched.

'Human beings are full of deceit,' Horse said. 'They flatter you with kind words but inside their thoughts are wicked. I understand your situation and I sympathise with you, but my experience with human beings has been quite unhappy. Everyone knows how gentle and humble I am, but see what they do to me even because of this. They climb upon my back and I carry them everywhere they want; and even when I am tired and cannot run very fast anymore, I am prodded in the side with sharp spikes, and whipped until I am sprinting again as if for my life. But sometimes when the suffering becomes unbearable, I throw the rider from my back in anger, and then they say Horse has without reason turned against them. I hate all human beings, and I want Leopard to eat you.' On hearing this Leopard again prepared to make a meal of Usman, but the man held up his hand.

'Three more to go,' he said to Leopard.

Soon they came to a mango tree and again Usman told the tree his tale of woe. And when he had finished, Tree said to him:

Usman took the door of the cage, shook it with all his might and saw that it was well locked.

'Very nice of you to tell me all this, but I can never say anything in support of a human being. They are all so arrogant. Here I stand everyday all by myself, doing nobody any harm, and when the sun is hot they come to sit at my foot and enjoy the peace around me. But when my fruits ripen, instead of them to climb gently up my branches and pick the fruits, the children throw sticks and stones at my branches and I lose so many leaves and my trunk became scarred. I think human beings are even more wicked than monkeys and surely Leopard must make an example of you and eat you today.'

Again Leopard bared his fangs, and raised his paws to tear Usman apart, but he also very quickly reminded:

'Two more persons to go.'

And so they went on along the bush path and soon came to a dog. As before, Usman told Dog his sorry tale. And again Dog, afraid that Leopard might be angry and eat him instead, advised that Leopard should not fail to make Usman its dinner on that very day.

'Eat him! Eat him! Eat him!' Dog barked; in fear of Leopard.

With Leopard licking his lips hungrily behind him, they finally came to a fox, who was now Usman's last hope of remaining alive. With tears in his eyes, Usman knelt and pleaded with Fox to save him.

'Dear Fox, I know that you are a very wise one, and so I plead with you to judge with true wisdom. I was minding my business and going to my farm when I saw Leopard in a steel cage. When I saw him I hurried away, but he called me and pleaded with me to have pity on him and to release him from the cage. I initially refused to do this because I feared that after he has become free, he might think to eat me. And it was as if I knew what was on his mind for immediately he had become free from the cage he leapt at me, held me by the neck and would have torn me to pieces and eaten me. But I pleaded with him to let this story be heard by five persons and that is why you find both of us standing before you. Please save me from this unhappy situation.'

After Usman had said this, Fox looked at him angrily.

'What was that all about?' Fox asked. 'I didn't even understand a word of your story at all. Don't you know that you are standing before the great Leopard? Are you not afraid to be in the presence of the great Leopard? If you want me to intervene in this matter, you must carefully and patiently tell me the story once more, because we are both standing before the great Leopard.'

And so Usman again told Fox the story. When he got to the part about the steel cage, Fox stopped him.

'One moment, what is a steel cage?' Fox asked.

'A cage made of steel,' Usman replied.

'Again I ask you what a steel cage is,' Fox impatiently asked. With hopes fading away Usman said:

'Fox, I know you are very wise, and I know for certain that if you do not know what a steel cage is, you do know what a chicken cage looks like, because you love eating chickens. And even before all this misfortune came upon me I had said to myself that on the day that I do meet Fox, I shall give him a gift of two or three fat chickens, because all the animals never stop saying good things about how good a person you are. But my promise will still one day be fulfilled; and even if Leopard kills me today, I shall still one day fulfil my promise and you will certainly get your three fat chickens. What do you want, hens or cockerels? The choice is yours. A steel cage and a chicken cage are not so different; but the steel cage is made of steel and it is much bigger than a chicken cage. I hope that you now understand, and I plead with you to have mercy and be fair in your judgment.' But Fox did not appear moved by Usman's story.

'What do you take me for then, a chicken thief?' Fox sneered. 'All you human beings think I am a chicken thief. You are a foolish fellow, like all of them. If you do not take me to the place where the steel cage is, I will not let you go away alive, because you are a liar and there was never any steel cage.' Again, Fox turned to Leopard and said to him:

'Hail, hail, O great Leopard. Anyone who has no respect for you should be forever known as a fool like this fellow standing before us. Please do not think it disrespectful if I ask that you come with us while this foolish fellow shows me where the steel cage can be found. I want him to see what a liar he is so that when I finally pass judgment that you should eat him there will be no doubt that I have been fair. And then I shall make sure that you eat him for dinner today.' And Leopard nodded in satisfaction.

'Thank you, Fox,' Leopard said. 'Let him lead and I will follow behind.'

When they got to the place where the steel cage was, Fox turned to Usman and sternly asked him.

'Where were you standing at that time?'

'There,' Usman replied pointing away from the cage.

'Okay stand there once again,' Fox said to him. Then Fox turned to Leopard and also asked:

'Where were you at that time sir?' And Leopard pointed at the cage.

'Inside there,' he told Fox. But Fox looked like he did not understand.

'Sir, I am sure that you do know how much like a child I am, and I never understand anything easily. If you do not stand where you were at that time, I am completely unable to understand.' So Leopard walked into the cage.

'Now it is becoming a little clearer to me,' Fox said.

'You liar, I thought you said you set him free? Tell me what prevents him from coming out of the cage by himself as the door is wide open?' Fox accused Usman.

'The door was locked at that time,' Usman desperately tried to explain.

'Locked? I am not very wise, what do you mean by locked?' Fox scolded. And so Usman took the door of the cage, slammed it shut and locked it.

'Locked like that,' he turned to Fox.

'Good, I now completely understand. Do you mean that Leopard cannot come out again now?' Fox asked. And so Usman took the door of the cage, shook it with all his might and saw that it was well locked.

'No, Leopard cannot come out by himself unless someone releases him,' Usman said to Fox. And so, Fox looked at Leopard in the cage and burst into laughter.

'Now who is the fool, Leopard? Again you are caught and this time there will be no escape because you have been unjust,' Fox taunted. And Leopard roared with rage and shook the steel cage with all his might but he was truly trapped again.

'Go on your way good man,' Fox said to Usman. 'But do not forget my chickens; and when you get to the nearest village, tell them that their enemy, Leopard, has been caught in a cage and they should come to kill him.'

And Usman thanked Fox very well, and went away to do as Fox had advised. Soon the villagers came and put Leopard to death, and while he died he thought: 'I should have lived more justly; else I wouldn't have died so unwisely.'

Questions:
1. Why is it good to be nice to animals and all other living things?
2. What does this story teach us? Choose one of following:

     i.   Not to help strangers.

    ii. Always to run away from leopards.

    iii. To give chickens to a fox.

    iv. Never to repay good with evil.

  3. What else does this story teach us?

Some Words and Their Meanings:

1. **Persuasive** – able to convince.
2. **Grudging** – reluctantly.
3. **Kids** – the children of a goat.
4. **Prodded** – jab with sharp object.
5. **Trunk** – body of a tree.
6. **Fangs** – sharp teeth of a wild animal or snake.
7. **Taunt** – tease.

THE LION'S FOOD

Once upon a time in a forest, there lived a lion, and it was the only lion in the forest. As the lion was getting too old he had knew that it would soon be too difficult to go hunting for food anymore. Therefore, he called all the animals in the forest together and spoke to them.

'I thank you all for coming and it shows that you love me and respect me as the king. I am sure that you also know that I am not a wicked king, because even if I have killed and eaten some of your fathers, mothers, brothers and sisters for dinner, you know that it was because you are all my food, even as some of you eat leaves, some eat fruits, and some eat nuts. Therefore, even though I must eat one of you every day, I also love you all. Therefore, I thought it a good idea to ask you all to put heads together and to come to me one at a time, one after the other to be eaten. In this way each of you will know which day they would die, and anyone of you whose death is near will spend the rest of their life more wisely. Again, I know how loudly I roar when I am hungry, and I am sure that this always makes you all afraid. If you come to me to be eaten my roaring will be unnecessary and there will be peace in the forest.'

After Lion had finished speaking there was a long silence. But Wolf soon stood and addressed them all again, saying:

'I am worried about a few things that the king said, especially the part about the type of food each of us eats. My suggestion is that when it is finally decided how each of you all will go to the king to be eaten, not all should go, because, I definitely eat nearly as much flesh as Lion, and I eat both from the forest from the villages around. Therefore one third of the animals for eating should come to me and the rest should go to Lion so that there will be peace in the forest.'

But Leopard rose up in disagreement.

'King Lion, your suggestion is so good, and I see some wisdom also in what Wolf has said. But if each of us makes such an argument as Wolf has done, I doubt if there will be any food left for the king to eat; because, if Wolf desires one third of the food, I think I should be entitled to half of all. I say this because my hunting skill is better that of Wolf. So few animals can match me for speed; and as for beauty, only Gazelle and Antelope, can really compete with me on that. How many animals have ever looked me in the eye and lived to tell the story?

I am as fearsome as even the king. I can eat a whole cow and that speaks for my appetite and how much food I need to eat. There are some of us who will not have to go to the king for eating; and I am speaking about persons like Elephant the mighty one of the forest; I, Leopard, the terror of the thickets; Wolf also may be forgiven. Apart from these three, every other animal should need to go to Lion to be eaten, and I suggest that Fox should be appointed to make a list of all animals that must go to be eaten and also the day each must go. I believe that Fox will do this well, because he is a very wise animal indeed.'

Elephant agreed, and so did the other animals. When Fox started to make a list of animals that shall be eaten by Lion, it was a surprise to all that he put his name first; but it was also comforting to all that Fox was not making any plan to escape their fate of being eaten by Lion. Thus by the register, it was the turn of Fox to be eaten the next morning.

But Fox failed to report to be eaten. The entire day passed and still Fox did not show up; and so Lion went hungry for that day. Very early the next morning, Lion called Elephant, Leopard and Wolf to an urgent meeting.

'Fox has failed to show up to be eaten even though his name was first on the list,' he complained. The other animals were also very surprised to hear this and they immediately sent for Fox.

'Why did you fail to come to be eaten?' they angrily asked him; and Fox knelt on the ground and begged.

'I pray that you will all live long, and I pray also that the hunters will never kill any of you. Forgive me, I meant no disrespect. How could I disrespect you when you have placed me in such a position of honour amongst all the other animals and to be appointed to prepare the king's food register? How could I repay the honour of becoming the first to be eaten by the king? But look at that Mahogany tree over there; that is where I live. At the tallest Iroko tree near the Mahogany, that is where I found four animals just like you all just yesterday; a lion, an elephant, a leopard and a wolf.

'They saw their reflections, but they thought
they were looking at four animals that looked
exactly like each of them.'

'And as I was coming to be eaten, they stopped me and ordered me to return home, and I am sure they will eventually do the same to all the other animals in the forest. Therefore, I say that until you remove them from this forest, there will not one single animal come to the king to be eaten.'

The four animals were surprised to learn that there were others in the same forest like them.

'Is it really true that there is another lion?' Lion asked greatly worried.

'Truly there is another; exactly like you,' Fox assured.

'Are you certain there is one?' Lion again asked, realising that another stronger lion in the forest meant that he would have to work even harder than before for his food.

'I have never told a lie in my life,' Fox replied. 'But one thing that I notice is that even though they are as big as each of you, they do not look as strong; because several times they have chased me and have never been able to catch me. I have no doubt in my heart that if you engage them in a fight, you will overcome them, and once you have killed them, all the other animals will joyfully take their turn to come to the king to be eaten.'

Fox had been so convincing and there seemed no doubt that he was telling the truth. And so the four animals rose and followed him to the place where the other trespassers were to be found. Fox led them to a large and deep well, which was full of water, and when they got there Fox pointed at the water.

'Look inside the hole and you will see the animals that I spoke of,' he said to them. And when the four animals looked, they saw their reflections, but they thought they were looking at four animals that looked exactly like each of them. They bared their teeth and snarled and the reflections did the same; they wagged their tails and so did the reflections.

'Let's go and get them,' Lion roared; and they all jumped inside the deep well and there perished.

Questions:
1. Why did the lion call all the other animals together?
2. What did the lion, elephant, wolf and leopard see inside the well?
3. This story teaches us not to be foolish. What else does this story teach us?

Some Words and Their Meanings:
1. **Skill** – ability to do something.
2. **Thicket** – bushes.
3. **Competition** – struggle to win something.

AJALA THE TERRIBLE CHILD

Once upon a time a woman had a baby boy, and he was a very lovely child. But no sooner had the child been born that he began to speak and to complain.

'Woe is me; so this is what life is all about. Why was I brought into this world; I never knew that it would be so as bad as it is here. Everywhere is so dirty and I certainly will not stay for long here.' And even as he finished saying this, he rose from his crib, went into the bathroom and washed himself thoroughly with soap and water. Then he covered himself with a soft warm blanket and sat on a chair. Not long after, he went into the kitchen, and ate six large loaves of bread, and he would have eaten more, only there was no more bread. And he came out from the kitchen crying because there was no more bread.

All these were unusual things for a baby to do, and soon people came from near and far to catch a glimpse of this miracle child, and he was very angry with them all.

On the seventh day when he was to be given a name, his parents prepared a feast for guests and very many were invited for the naming ceremony.

'My name is Ajala,' he said to all of them when it was time to give him a name. And everyone was so amazed.

Now when the food for the feast was being cooked in the kitchen, Ajala had ceaselessly complained. He complained about the food, he complained about the cooks, he complained about how slow they all were. After a while he found a ladle and began to stir the stew in the fire, to the utter surprise and annoyance of the cooks.

'What a horrible child,' they all complained. And when he heard this he found a whip and beat them all so severely that they fled the kitchen and the house. And even when the feast had begun, he still remained angry. He again found the whip and beat the guests so much that they fled in all directions, and he ran after them and whipped them all along the way. It was a day of great confusion.

After the guests had all gone away, he returned home.

'I heard that you are all so foolish, but never mind I will make you wise,' he shouted after them. And even as he said this, he went into his mother's room and broke six of her best dishes; then he went into the garden and trampled six large chickens to death.

'This is a really dreadful child,' a bystander said to himself. Ajala slapped him six times on the face, so hard that the man lost six teeth. As they wrestled, another man tried to stop the fight, but Ajala kicked him six times, so hard that the man fell down unconscious. Looking over his shoulder, he saw a group of men watching a game of draughts, and so he abandoned the fight, took over the draughts challenge and won six games in a row. His older brother watching all this was so amazed, he opened his mouth too wide and his face split right to the back of his head. And so did Ajala become a terror to all.

All this continued for a whole month, of which the entire town lived in terror of Ajala, and it became known that it was dangerous for anyone to cross this terrible child.

There was a very powerful *Babalawo* in this town and he was indeed widely known for his healing skill. Ever since he had heard about this terrible child, he had boasted:

'He's only a difficult child; troubled by terrible spirits no doubt, but on the very day that I meet him face to face, he will be cured.'

And so, one day the *Babalawo* dressed himself up in his magic charms and in black battle dress and headed for Ajala's house. When he got there, he found Ajala eating, but he paid no attention to the child. He went to the mother who sadly sat watching from a distance. It was quite an astonishing sight indeed to see Ajala eating, for he had enough food on his enormous plate to feed ten men, and his spoon was almost as large as a shovel. Clearly nobody could eat from the same plate with this terrible child. As the *Babalawo* and Ajala's mother spoke with each other they came to mention the child's name in their conversation. When Ajala heard this, he stood and hurled a large piece of yam in the *Babalawo*'s face. Then he took his bowl of stew and emptied it upon the man's head. Even as the *Babalawo* sat surprised and dumbstruck, Ajala took hold of his robe and tore it apart, and then he seized the *Babalawo*'s bag of magic charms and whipped him over the head with it, so hard that the bag was torn into shreds; and the *Babalawo* wept and screamed for mercy.

The Babalawo found a way to escape and fled
the house; but Ajala chased after him.

Somehow the *Babalawo* found a way to escape and fled the house; but Ajala chased after him all the way to his home, before returning to his lunch. The *Babalawo*, his body covered in sores, and left with only his trousers looked a sorry sight indeed.

'What happened to you?' people came from all over to ask the *Babalawo*.

'That child is extremely terrible,' the *Babalawo* wept. 'Ever since I was born I have never met with as much misery as I did today. I have never been beaten so much in my life. That child nearly flogged me to death.'

'Was it that bad?' one of his friends asked. 'Did you not take all your magic charms with you?'

'What magic charms,' the *Babalawo* sneered. 'He took them all away.'

'What about your clothes? Did you go there naked? Did he also take away your cap?' Someone else wanted to know; and the *Babalawo* was very angry.

'Stop asking me foolish questions,' he shouted at them. 'Did I not just tell you how he took all my clothes and magic charms away, and here you stand asking me about my cap. If I did not run, do you think he would not have taken my trousers too? If there is any more of you going the way of that terrible child's house, my advice to you is to make sure that if you do meet him, run as fast as you can else your death is near. And if you do come running to my house I will certainly push you out into the street,' he advised them.

So did Ajala become to be known as a terror at home and in the streets; and so much that his mother was no more able to bear the disgrace. Therefore one day, she took Ajala with her on a journey through a forest, and midway she told him to wait for her, while she goes to bathe in the river. But she headed back home instead, leaving Ajala all alone in the forest and there was not another soul in sight.

As Ajala wandered about in the forest, he found five animals living happily together. They were an elephant, a lion, a leopard, a wolf and a goat. When he got to them, Ajala pleaded to be allowed to live with them and to be their servant; and they agreed.

It was the duty of one of the animals to go out to look for food each day, and they all shared this task. When any of them went out on a particular day, the rest would remain home and when the food came, they would all share it. This was how they had lived in harmony for many years until Ajala came. As he was still a guest Ajala behaved himself on this night and was very pleasant to all.

Next morning, Lion gathered all of them together.

'Now that we have a servant, I suggest that every day when each of us goes out to look for food, our servant should go along.'

And all the other animals, including Ajala, also thought that this was a very good suggestion.

It was Goat's duty to look for food on this day. Therefore when Goat set out to hunt for food, Ajala went along. But as Goat searched for food, Ajala played. However, Goat left him in peace; after all, he was a mere child and not wise yet, Goat thought. After he had put all the food in a sack, Goat called Ajala to help lift it onto his back. But when Ajala got to Goat, he seized Goat by the legs, pushed him to the ground and began to kick him until Goat's face was swollen all over. Goat shouted for help but there was nobody near. Ajala beat him to an inch of his life.

'When we get home, if you tell anyone that I beat you I shall certainly kill you,' Ajala warned after he finally left Goat alone.

After Goat had stopped crying and brushed the dust off his body, he lifted the sack of food onto his back and headed for home; and Ajala followed behind whistling cheerfully. They soon got home, and when the others saw Goat's swollen face, they were so alarmed.

'What on earth did this to you?' Lion demanded. But Goat did not dare tell them the truth.

'When I was looking for food, I came across a bee hive and the bees stung me all over the head. And as I ran, I fell upon a wasps' nest and they again stung me from head to hoof. That is why my face and eyes are so swollen,' Goat lied.

Next day, it was Wolf's turn to go hunting for food, and Ajala again went along with him. When Wolf came home in the evening, his face was also swollen and his body covered with sores.

'What on earth did this to you?' Lion again sought to know.

'What happened to Goat yesterday also happened to me, and I think it shall certainly happen to all of us,' Wolf said with a bitter laugh. Wolf's eyes met with Goat's and both sadly shook their heads, but Ajala whistled nonchalantly.

So did Ajala with all the animals until it became Lion's turn to go hunting for food. After

Lion had also been beaten nearly to death, Lion gathered the rest to a secret meeting that night.

'Let us run away and leave the terrible child behind,' Goat desperately advised.

'Yes, let us run away before dawn and before he wakes up,' the rest of them agreed. Therefore in the night they packed their belongings into a cart and prepared to quietly sneak away at dawn. But while they planned, little did they know that Ajala had been listening. And when Ajala saw that they had gone to sleep, he hid himself inside the cart in which they had packed their belongings. This was not too difficult, because Ajala was no more than a foot and a half tall.

Before day broke, the animals quietly left the house and they headed for deep inside the forest, running away from Ajala. After a while Goat got hungry and planned to steal some of the food inside the cart.

'Go on in front of me, I need to rest for a few minutes,' Goat told the others; but it was a lie and all he wanted to do was steal some of the food in the cart. After they had gone, Goat began to look for the food box that was inside the cart. But out jumped Ajala and beat him so much that Goat would never forget this day for the rest of his life. Finally, he stopped beating Goat and as before warned him to say nothing about what had happened.

'When you catch up with the others give the cart to Wolf, and let me see whether he is also as foolish as you,' Ajala told Goat.

Goat ran with the cart and soon caught up with the others, and gave the cart to Wolf.

'I am weary, take this cart for a while,' he said to Wolf, who agreed. Soon after Wolf also thought to stay behind and steal some of the food in the cart. Ajala again seized him and Wolf had never suffered so much in his life as he did on this day. He could have screamed to call his friends for help him but Ajala held him by the neck and would have strangled him. It was a terrible day for Wolf. When Ajala was tired, he let Wolf go. Again he told Wolf to hand the cart over to someone else when he caught up with the rest. This was how this terrible child tormented the animals that were running away from him. Elephant was the last to fall into his hands, but as he took hold of Elephant by the ears, Elephant trumpeted in fear and fled after the rest and together they raced madly away with Ajala in hot pursuit.

In utter fear the animals cried aloud as they fled and the forest echoed their cries and footfall. But Ajala was wiser; he took a shorter route and arrived ahead of them further up the forest path.

Then he found a leafy tree, and climbed up this tree to wait for the fleeing animals. They soon arrived, even as he had expected, quite exhausted.

'He is no more chasing after us. I think he's gone away, let us rest in the shade of this tree,' Wolf said. All the others agreed; and as they rested they cursed and insulted Ajala.

'We would not have been in this terrible situation, if Goat had not asked that we allow the little demon to stay with us,' Wolf accused; but Goat denied.

'Shut up, or I will trample you to death,' Elephant warned Goat.

'And remember, all that running has made me very hungry right now and goat meat sounds delicious,' Lion growled at Goat. But Goat rose and nonetheless made a passionate defence of himself.

'If it was I who suggested that Ajala be permitted to live with us, let the ground open and swallow me up. But if it wasn't me, let that same terrible wind that brought Ajala into our midst bring him again this very instant,' Goat swore. When Ajala heard this, he gleefully jumped down from the tree into their midst, and again they fled for their lives. And since that day Goat fled to the safety of places where human beings live; Elephant fled to Africa and to India, Leopard and Wolf fled deeper into the jungle and Lion into the grasslands.

What happened to Ajala thereafter? Did he begin to wander ceaselessly in the jungle? No, God saw that Ajala did not like anything about the world or anyone in the world, even as he had said when he was born. So God sent for Ajala to be brought back from the world.

Questions:
1. How many loaves of bread did Ajala eat on the day he was born?
2. How big was Ajala's spoon?
3. How tall was Ajala?
4. What animals did Ajala meet in the forest?
5. This story teaches us not to be bad children. What else does this story teach us?

Some Words and Their Meanings:
1. **Woe is me**! – a cry of sorrow.
2. **Crib** – the bed of a baby.
3. **Dreadful** – terrible.
4. **Babalawo** – a Yoruba native healer.
5. **Dumbstruck** – unable to talk.
6. **Tormented** – constantly attacked.
7. **Leafy** – having plenty of leaves.
8. **Trample** - walk over.

THE FOOLISH RICH MAN

Chief Emeka was a rich man, and he was indeed so prosperous that he was the richest man in his town. But Chief Emeka was also very bad tempered; always angry and never forgave anyone who offended him. Despite this he never failed to go to church every Sunday.

One Sunday morning while in church, the organ playing so beautifully, the singing choir came to the chorus part of a very sweet hymn which Chief Emeka loved so much, even though he did not know what the chorus was about because the song was in a language which he did not understand. But this morning, he turned to the person sitting next to him and asked.

'What does that chorus say?' His neighbour was very pleased to be of help.

'The song says:

He removes the rich from their mansions,
And he lifts up the poor.'

The neighbour told him. And when Chief Emeka heard this, he was very angry. So angry was he that he wished he had a gun to shoot the organist, or a sword to kill the entire choir.

'Remind me when church is over to teach these nasty people a lesson that they will never forget for the rest of their lives,' he said. 'Now I know why they sing songs in a language that I do not understand. It is just to insult me. Who is richer than me in this town or for miles beyond? Does God not have his kingdom up there in heaven and I mine here on earth. I am not able to remove God from his heaven, and neither can he remove me from my mansion.'

And when God heard all that Emeka had said, He smiled and said to one of the angels that stood around Him:

'Hear what this fool has said. After I have given him so much food and so much pleasant drinks, and he has become content, he forgets where it all came from. Every day, fools like this make themselves equal to me; but do I get angry and immediately punish them? No, I have pity on them and remember that I created them imperfect. If I should wish to reward him as I should for his folly, what am I not able to do with him?'

'Change him into an animal or a tree; turn him into a beast,' one of the angels suggested.

'Give him a punishment that nobody has even seen before,' another said. But God shook His head.

'I will not do any of these. Angel, I want you to go to him and just take away those things which have made him so proud. Do not harm him in any way. I want you to give him a chance to repent, and when he has done so I want you to give them back to him.'

And when the angel heard this, he did as God had ordered. Within minutes after Chief Emeka had spoken in the church where he sat, the angel came to him and made him to fall asleep. After this the angel turned Chief Emeka's rich clothes into rags and his gold ornaments into rusted tin plates. Then the angel changed his own appearance to be exactly like Chief Emeka and made Chief Emeka to look like a dirty beggar. The angel then moved Chief Emeka to a pew at the back of the church and thereafter sat in his place. All this happened without anyone noticing and within a second.

When the church service was over everyone went to their homes and the church doors were shut. In the middle of the night Chief Emeka finally woke up inside the dark church. He felt his way around in the darkness stumbling over pews and other furniture. Soon he found the church doors and started to beat it with his fist and with all his might and to shout for help. The church guard heard, and he opened the door to see what was going on. What he saw was a dirty man covered with rags. And the guard fled, thinking Chief Emeka might be a dangerous lunatic. Chief Emeka did not understand what it was that had made the man to run away from him, because as far as he could see nothing had changed about him. Indeed, when he looked at himself in a glass window, he still saw himself dressed in the beautiful clothes that he had in the morning worn to church.

Chief Emeka hurried away to his mansion. When he got to the gate his found it locked, but he knew that there were guards on the other side. Hadn't he employed them?

'Open up the gate,' Chief Emeka shouted, as he hammered impatiently on the gate with his fist.

'Who are you?' the guards on the other side shouted back.

'It's a mad man, and it looks like he has been mad even before my mother was born.'

'I am your master,' he shouted back. But the guards on the other side only laughed when they heard this.

'Stupid man; he must be drunk,' they said to one another; and Chief Emeka was furious.

'Who are you calling a drunk? I will make you regret what you have just said when morning comes.' And because he worried them for so long, one of the guards opened the gate a little to catch a glimpse of who it was that has been making them to laugh so much. But the guard quickly shut the gate again.

'It's a mad man, and it looks like he has been mad even before my mother was born. If anyone of you dares to venture outside there, your life is finished,' he warned. And this was how Chief Emeka spent the rest of the cold night outside the gate of his own mansion.

When it was morning, the guards permitted him into the mansion and took him to see their master. And when the angel saw Chief Emeka, he was filled with pity and he ordered that his rags be changed.

'He's not a lunatic, I think he's a jester,' the angel said. And from that day, Chief Emeka was employed as a jester in the mansion, and given a small room in the servants' quarters.

Many months passed, and nothing changed for Emeka the jester, even though he still thought all this misfortune that had happened to him a dream. How else could he have become a jester in his own mansion? All his days were spent in sorrow and in reflection. But one day, Emeka realised where he had gone wrong and he was struck by the fear of God.

The next Sunday, he arrived at the church even before the first bell rang. And there he knelt at the altar and prayed for forgiveness. When the church service began, he again listened to the choir's song hoping to hear that beautiful chorus -

'He removes the rich from their mansions,
And he lifts up the poor.'

And when the choir began to sing the chorus, Chief Emeka sang with all his might; and his voice was heard all around the church; so much that the entire congregation laughed at the shouting jester. But he paid them no attention.

'Next week I shall sing even louder,' he said to them. After the church service was over and everyone had gone to their separate homes, Chief Emeka waited behind, and again he went to the altar and there knelt and prayed for forgiveness, and for a long time before leaving for his small room at the servants' quarters of his mansion.

Shortly after Chief Emeka arrived home, the angel sent for him. When he got there, the angel ordered everyone else to leave the room. Then the angel stood and closed all the doors and windows, and the room was in total darkness. Chief Emeka waited in the darkness, not knowing what to expect. Soon he heard sound, of marching feet all around and they were so many that the floor and walls of the mansion shook. A strong wind blew through the dark room even though all doors and windows were shut, then as sudden as it had all begun, the noises stopped and the room was filled with a brilliant light. And when Chief Emeka lifted his face he saw the angel floating above, his robe brilliant white and his eyes bright like diamonds; and Chief Emeka was extremely afraid. He fell to the floor and covered his face.

'I am one of the seven angels that stand before God,' the angel said. 'After you have eaten and drank your fill, you forgot that you did not create yourself and not even the food and drink. And you began to speak without wisdom. But God saw and ordered me to take away your pride until you have repented. I see now that you have found wisdom and I command that you be restored to your position. But remember, if you fail to use it wisely, you will lose it again.'

And when the angel had said this, he disappeared. Chief Emeka found himself once more in his rich clothes as on the day that the misfortune had befallen him.

Questions

1. What did the angel turn Chief Emeka into?

2. What did Chief Emeka do to return to his former position?

3. This story teaches us not to be arrogant. What else does this story teach us?

Some Words and Their Meanings:

1. **Organ** – a musical instrument which looks like a piano.

2. **Choir** – a group of singers, especially in a church.

3. **Chorus** – the part of a song which is sung together by several people or by a choir.

4. **Beast** – animal.

5. **Pew** – wooden bench in a church.

6. **Lunatic** – a mad person.

7. **Jester** – a person who makes people laugh.

8. **Mansion** – a big house.

www.ingramcontent.com/pod-product-compliance
Lightning Source LLC
Chambersburg PA
CBHW070811120626
46557CB00002B/811